S0-BMR-688

THIS BOOK IS BASED ON THE REAL LIFE STORY OF MARY RODAS. MARY CONTINUES TO WORK WITH THE INVENTOR AND MR. BALZAC TO DEVELOP PRODUCTS THAT MAKE KIDS HAPPY, AND WITH THOSE LESS FORTUNATE THAN SHE TO MAKE THEIR LIVES A LITTLE BETTER. SHE TRULY IS AN EXAMPLE OF THE AMERICAN DREAM COME TRUE.

COPYRIGHT © 1995 CATCO INC.

PUBLISHED BY CATCO INC.
ALL RIGHTS RESERVED. NO PART OF THIS BOOK MAY BE
REPRODUCED OR TRANSMITTED IN ANY FORM OR BY ANY
MEANS, ELECTRONIC OR MECHANICAL, INCLUDING
PHOTOCOPYING, RECORDING OR BY ANY INFORMATION
STORAGE AND RETRIEVAL SYSTEM, WITHOUT PERMISSION
IN WRITING FROM CATCO INC., NEW YORK, NEW YORK 10010

TEXT AND ILLUSTRATIONS BY DEREK WEISHAUPT

FIRST EDITION
PRINTED IN THE UNITED STATES OF AMERICA

LIBRARY OF CONGRESS CATALOG CARD NUMBER: 95-69719

ISBN 0-9647068-0-6

HIYA KIDS! MR. BALZAC'S THE NAME AND I'M HERE TO TELL YA A LITTLE STORY. THAT'S RIGHT, IT'S THE STORY OF A LITTLE GIRL AND A BALL. NOT JUST ANY BALL, BUT A MAGIC BALL THAT CHANGED HER LIFE FOREVER. IT ALL STARTED LONG AGO...

IT WAS AMERICA! THE LAND OF FREEDOM! THE HOME OF THE BRAVE! THE LAND OF OPPORTUNITY, NOT TO MENTION GREAT PIZZA! FOR YOUNG MIGUEL AND MARINA IT WAS ALSO THEIR NEW HOME.

THEY CAME ALL THE WAY FROM EL SALVADOR. THAT'S IN CENTRAL AMERICA. THEY CAME TO THE UNITED STATES TO BUILD THEIR DREAMS. MIGUEL WORKED AS A HANDYMAN IN THE BUILDING WHERE THEY LIVED. MARINA GOT WORK AS A MAID.

ONE DAY, WHEN MARY WAS FOUR YEARS OLD, SHE WENT WITH HER POP TO REPAIR ONE OF THE APARTMENTS IN THEIR BUILDING. THE NICE MAN WHO LIVED THERE WAS AN INVENTOR. HE HAD JUNK ALL OVER THE PLACE. BUT IT WAS FUN JUNK.

THE INVENTOR AND MARY BECAME BEST FRIENDS. HE KNEW SHE HAD A GREAT GIFT. THAT GIFT WAS A WONDERFUL IMAGINATION.

MARY AND THE INVENTOR SPENT MANY HOURS WORKING ON THE INVENTIONS. THEY WORKED UNTIL THEY WERE HAPPY WITH WHAT THEY HAD DONE, OR UNTIL THEY GOT REALLY HUNGRY FOR CHEESEBURGERS.

AT NIGHT, MARY WOULD DREAM ABOUT THE TOYS SHE CREATED. SHE DREAMT ABOUT LOTS OF CHILDREN LAUGHING AND PLAYING WITH ALL THE DIFFERENT TOYS. THIS MADE HER VERY HAPPY.

OTH OF MARY'S
ARENTS WORKED
ERY HARD DURING
HE DAY. A LOT OF
IMES LITTLE MARY
OUND HERSELF
ITTING HOME
LONE AFTER
CHOOL. THIS
GAVE MARY MORE TIME
O SPEND WITH THE
NVENTOR WORKING
ON THE TOYS.

MONTHS PASSED AND MARY'S MOTHER BECAME
VERY SICK. MARY WAS SO SAD THAT HER SCHOOL-
WORK BEGAN TO SUFFER AND HER GRADES BEGAN
TO DROP. THE INVENTOR WAS
SAD TOO. HE WANTED TO DO
SOMETHING NICE FOR MARY.

THE KIND INVENTOR TOLD MARY'S MOTHER, "IF THINGS GET ANY WORSE, I WILL ALWAYS BE THERE TO HELP LITTLE MARY, ANY WAY THAT CAN." THIS MADE MARY'S MOTHER SMILE.

MARY'S MOTHER PASSED AWAY SHORTLY AFTER. MARY WAS VERY SAD. SHE WAS SITTING ALONE IN HER ROOM CRYING WHEN, SUDDENLY, SHE NOTICED THE UGLY GRAY BALL WAS GLOWING. THE BALL STARTED BOUNCING UP AND DOWN, OVER AND UNDER, SIDE TO SIDE. IT EVEN BOUNCED OFF MARY'S HEAD. THIS MADE HER LAUGH!

"YOU SURE ARE AN UGLY BALL," SAID MARY. "BUT YOU'RE LOTS AND LOTS OF FUN!" THEN MARY HAD A GREAT IDEA. SHE PULLED OUT AN OLD BOX THAT HER MOTHER HAD GIVEN HER FOR CHRISTMAS. INSIDE WAS A BEAUTIFUL CLOTH WITH LOTS OF NEW COLORS. SHE WRAPPED THE CLOTH AROUND THE UGLY GRAY BALL. "NOW YOU ARE BEAUTIFUL!" SAID MARY.

THE NEXT MORNING WHEN MARY WOKE UP, SHE COULDN'T BELIEVE HER EYES. HER ROOM WAS FILLED WITH THE COLORS OF THE BALL, LIKE THE BEDROOM OF A BEAUTIFUL PRINCESS! MARY QUIETLY WHISPERED, "WOW!"

THE MAGIC BALL BEGAN BOUNCING AGAIN. AROUND THE ROOM. OUT THE DOOR DOWN THE HALLWAY. AS IT BOUNCED, THE WHOLE BUILDING STARTED TO COME ALIVE WITH WONDERFUL COLORS! THE BIG BEAUTIFUL BALL ROLLED INTO THE INVENTOR'S APARTMENT.

MARY AND THE INVENTOR DECIDED TO TAKE THE MAGIC BALL TO THE HOSPITAL TO SEE IF SOME OF THE SICK CHILDREN MIGHT HAVE SOME FUN WITH THEIR NEW TOY.

AND BOY OH BOY DID THEY EVER. THEIR FACES LIT UP LIKE A BRIGHT SUNNY MORNING. THEY GIGGLED AND PLAYED ALL DAY LONG. THE BALL HAD WORKED IT'S MAGIC AGAIN!

THEY DECIDED TO CALL
THE MAGIC BALL, BALZAC.
THAT'S MY NAME MR. BALZAC!
AND THE BALL BEGAN TO
POP UP ALL OVER THE WORLD
IN ALL DIFFERENT SIZES AND
COLORS. SMALL ONES, BIG ONES.
ONES THAT LOOKED FUNKY.
ONES THAT LOOKED LIKE
THE WORLD. EVERBODY LOVED
THE BALZAC BALLOON BALL.
LITTLE KIDS, TEENAGERS,
EVEN ADULTS! YOU NAME IT!

MARY'S PICTURE WAS IN THE NEWSPAPER AND SHE EVEN APPEARED ON TELEVISION. SHE WAS FAMOUS! IT WAS A DREAM COME TRUE. THE BALZAC BALLOON BALL WAS BRINGING HAPPINESS ALL OVER THE WORLD!

LITTLE MARY BECAME RICH AND FAMOUS. SHE USED HER MONEY AND HER TREMENDOUS TALENTS TO HELP THOSE PEOPLE WHO WERE LESS FORTUNATE. SHE WORKED WITH HOSPITALS, SCHOOLS, AND MANY ORGANIZATIONS ALL OVER THE WORLD HELPING CHILDREN AND OTHERS IN NEED.

Mary Rodas